Little Skaters

A Grosset & Dunlap ALL ABOARD BOOK®

To Connor and Kerry: May they always love to skate—N.S.

Special thanks to Kathy Cadwell, the Faillace family, parents,
assistants, and especially the little skaters.

Thanks also to "After the Stork" for children's clothes, and Karen Biggins of Birch Hill Designs, Inc., for skating costumes.

Library of Congress Cataloging-in-Publication Data

Morris, Ann, 1930-
   Little skaters / by Ann Morris ; photographs by Nancy Sheehan.
   p. cm.—(A Grosset & Dunlap all aboard book)
   Summary: Describes the experience of ice skating, from lacing up your very first skates to putting on a show.
   1. Skating—Juvenile literature. 2. Skaters—Juvenile literature. [1. Ice skating.] I. Sheehan, Nancy, ill. II. Title. III. Series.
GV849.M67 1997
796.91—dc21   97-18136
                                                                                                                CIP
ISBN 0-448-41734-0   A B C D E F G H I J   AC

Little Skaters

By Ann Morris
Photographs by Nancy Sheehan

Grosset & Dunlap, Publishers

It's a special day for Cindy. She's getting her first pair of ice skates!

Cindy's dad checks to be sure the skates fit. He shows her how to lace them up tight so she won't wobble on the ice. Cindy can't wait to try them out!

Near Cindy's house, there is a pond where everyone goes to skate. Cindy goes the very next morning. She is glad nobody else is there yet. She has the pond all to herself.

While her dad watches, Cindy steps onto the ice. Her new skates sparkle.

"They're perfect!" says Cindy.

"Whoops!" When Cindy tries to skate, she takes a flop. Skating is not easy. Cindy is ready for some skating lessons.

Kathy is Cindy's skating teacher. She teaches lots of other children, too.

All the children love Kathy. She makes them laugh. She is patient while they are learning.

The first thing she teaches them is how to fall down safely.

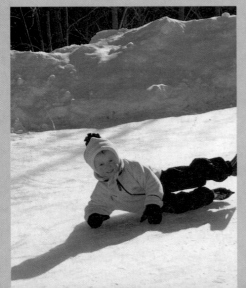

They never knew that falling could be such fun—
that is, when it's done the right way!

The children try skating on their own. All the moms and dads come to watch. Everybody is dressed in warm jackets and snow pants, woolly hats, scarves, and gloves.

It feels so good to be outdoors on the ice and in the snow!

But it's cold. Brr-r-r! The children take time out for hot cocoa.

They have fun in the snow with their friends, and with their families, too.

Then Kathy calls out, "Let's make a circle. We can warm up to the hokeypokey."
Doing the hokeypokey is tricky on ice skates!

"Let's make a snake," says Kathy. "Hold on!
Now everybody follow the leader!"

There are some older children at the pond who have been skating for a long time. They help the little skaters.

"C'mon, you can do it," they say. "Here, hold my hand. Try it like this. Good for you!"

They teach the little skaters how to glide and slide, and turn and twirl. There is a lot to learn. The little skaters come for lessons every week. They practice all winter long.

Pretty soon they can do things they couldn't do before. They can skate on one leg...

...and bend a knee.

They can even make a perfect pinwheel. It's time for them to show their moms and dads what they have learned. Kathy is going to have everybody perform in an ice-skating show!

At home, Cindy tells her doll all about the show.
"One day you'll be a good skater, too," she says. "I'll teach you."
At night, she and her friends make pretty pom-poms to tie onto their skates. The pom-poms match their new skating costumes.

On the morning of the show, it is snowing.

Cindy and her dad make pancakes for breakfast. They will give her lots of energy.

"Mm-m, good!" says Cindy. She eats her pancakes in a hurry so they can be on their way. She is eager to show her dad what she can do.

Meanwhile, at the pond, the snow must be shoveled away so the skaters will have smooth ice to skate on.

Cindy arrives dressed up
in her skating costume—
pom-poms and all.

Everyone comes in their
costumes. They are ready.

They put on a wonderful show!
And when the show is over...

...Kathy gives each of them a surprise.
    "Everyone gets a silver skate pin to wear!"
says Kathy. "I'm so proud of all my little skaters!"